1-2-3
peas

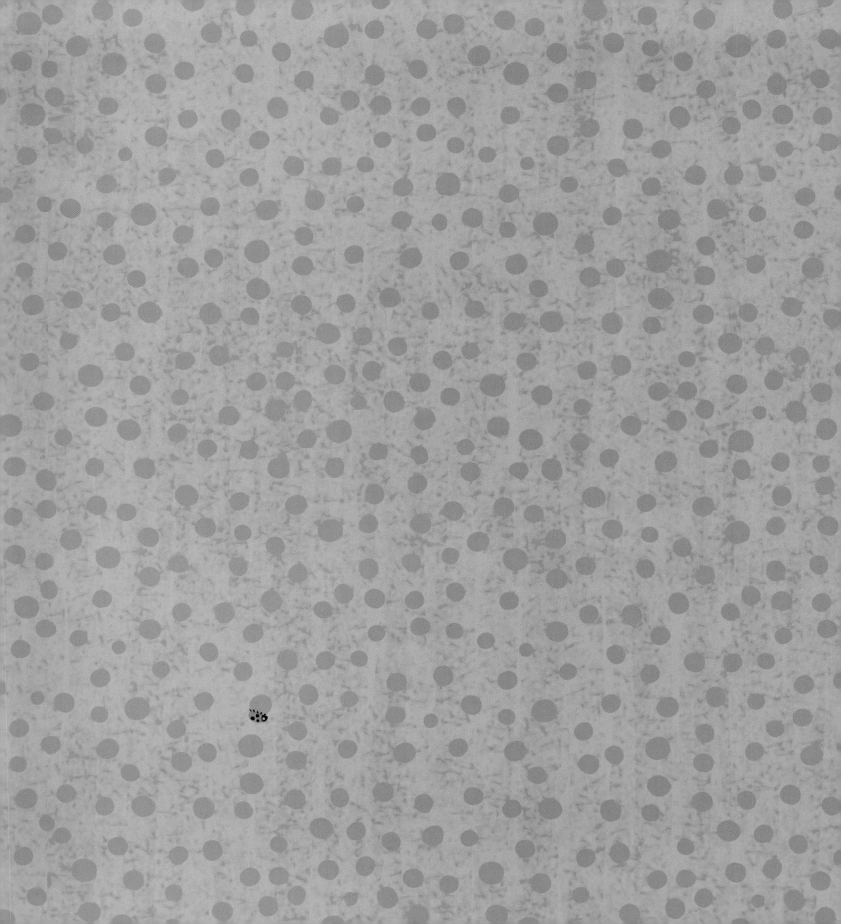

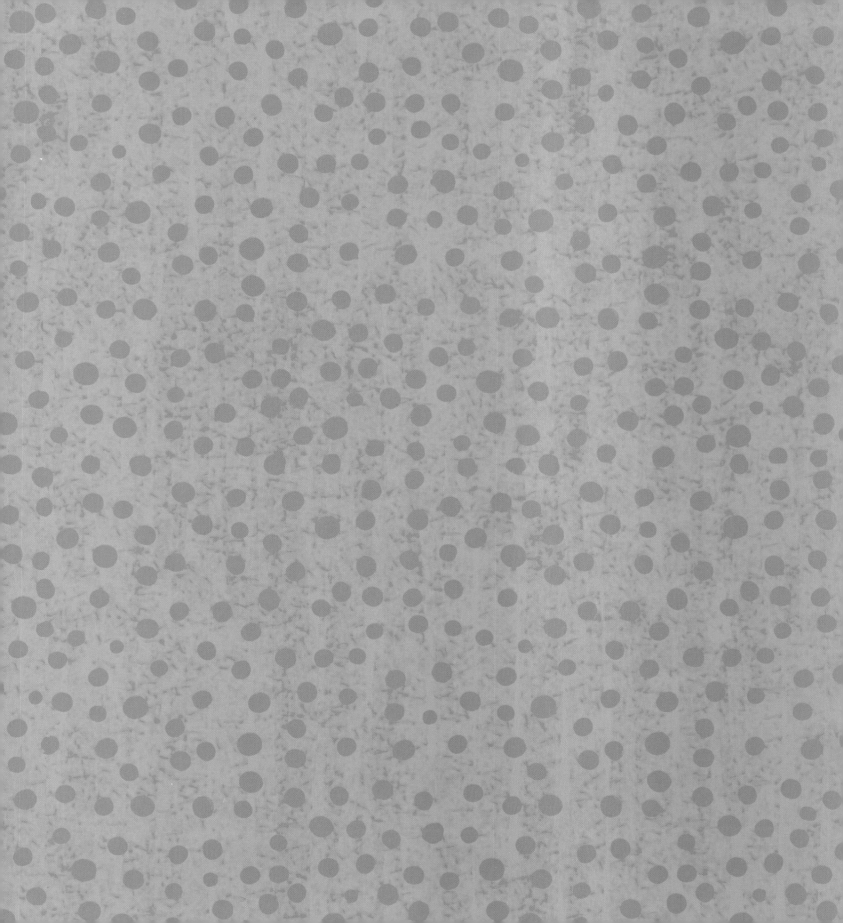

For my mother and father—*love, love, love!*

ISBN 978-0-545-62076-5

Copyright © 2012 by Keith Baker.
All rights reserved. Published by Scholastic Inc., 557 Broadway, New York, NY 10012, by arrangement with Beach Lane Books, an imprint of Simon & Schuster Children's Publishing Division. SCHOLASTIC and associated logos are trademarks and/or registered trademarks of Scholastic Inc.

15 14 13   19 20 21/0

Printed in the U.S.A.   40

First Scholastic printing, September 2013

Book design by Sonia Chaghatzbanian
The text for this book is set in Frankfurter Medium.
The illustrations for this book are rendered digitally.

Keith Baker

1-2-3 peas

SCHOLASTIC INC.

1 ONE

pea searching—
look, look, look,

TWO
peas fishing—
hook, hook, hook.

2

3

THREE
peas boating—
row, row, row,

FOUR

peas planting—
grow, grow, grow.

FIVE

peas painting—
brush, brush, brush,

6

SIX peas traveling—
rush, rush, rush.

S
E
V
E
N

peas jumping—
splash, splash, splash!

EIGHT

peas racing—*dash, dash, dash.*

peas dancing—*round, round, round,*

TEN

peas building—
pound, pound, pound.

Eleven to nineteen—*skip, skip, skip!*

TWENTY

peas cutting—*snip, snip, snip.*

THIRTY

peas honking—
beep, beep, beep!

FORTY

peas napping—
sleep, sleep, sleep.

SIXTY

peas watching— *wow, wow, wow!*

SEVENTY

peas singing— *la, la, la,*

NINETY

peas floating—*free, free, free,*

ONE

peas counting, *hap-pea as can be. . . .*

Please count again with us!